The Real Life Adventures of Anna and Saddie

Christina

Dean Balderston, MA Ed. LMHP

authorHOUSE®

AuthorHouse™
1663 Liberty Drive, Suite 200
Bloomington, IN 47403
www.authorhouse.com
Phone: 1-800-839-8640

First published by AuthorHouse 2/10/2009

ISBN: 978-1-4343-7620-6 (sc)

Printed in the United States of America
Bloomington, Indiana

This book is printed on acid-free paper.

Contents

Acknowledgments

I would like to extend a sincere thank you to:

Those who were the first to review this book; your opinions, editing, and help are greatly appreciated: Michelle Bruha, Nancy Welniak, Sara Case, Kathy Bruha and Dr. Lisa Pattison Psy. D.

I also want to thank all of you who believed in me: Mike Pop, Mike Kriefels, Randy Weverka and Brian Balderston.

All of my clients, past and present.

All my friends at KNLV radio station: John Bish, Walt Smith, James King, Gene McCoy, Denise O'Neel, Jeannie Neidhardt and Paul Harkness.

The guys and gals at the Bus Shop: Amber Severence, Dani Hunt, Jerry Bauer, Don Proskocil, Bill Longo, Larry Schweitzer, Kim Musil

Thank you to the following special group of kids: Erin, Janae, Tom, Jacob, Jeff, Evan, Cali, Courtney, Rachel, Tate, Michaela, Joseph, Morgan, Cody, Carissa, McKenna, Chandler, and Riley.

A special thank you to the following people, whose journeys into self-discovery have touched my soul and have been a wonderful inspiration. If not for your willingness to share the pain and torment of your healing journeys, I would not have persevered: Angela Shelton, Dave Pelzer and Lynn Tolsen

Dedication

To the most important person in my life—my wonderful son, Brian. I love you, bud; you will always have my heart. Thank you for putting up with me when I stressed and for hanging in there when we didn't always get to play the Playstation when you wanted to.

Chapter 1

Getting Ready for School

October can be a chilly and rainy month in Nebraska, and this year is no exception. It has been raining for several days, but that hasn't affected the mood of the family that resides at 456 South D Street in Ord, Nebraska. Ms. Sarah Allen finds herself busy as usual this morning. Sarah, a thirty-one-year-old single mother of two, works at Good Humanitarian Hospital as a registered nurse. Because she must wear a nurse's hat she keeps her long blonde hair pulled back. She keeps fit for work by joining the women's softball, volleyball and basketball league every year at the local YWCA. Sarah's ability to be patient comes in handy on this day like many others. Attempting to get both of her daughters, Anna and Saddie, ready for school and get herself off to work at the same time proves to be stressful.

Anna, at thirteen, is the older of the two Allen sisters. She is tall and attractive with blue eyes, high cheekbones, slight dimples that she inherited from her mother, and long blond hair. She appears older than she really is and receives a lot of attention for it, especially from older boys. Although she likes boys, she's not quite ready for that kind of attention and simply ignores it.

Saddie, the youngest at nine, has shoulder-length strawberry-blond hair, sparkling blue eyes, and more pronounced dimples than Anna. She is very pretty, and she knows it. Sometimes that is an unfortunate thing, as Saddie wants things her way or no way at all and uses her looks to achieve that goal. Despite this, Saddie is a very caring person and demands that others are cared for. She is athletic and very competitive and has a tendency to spend her time with the boys, playing football and other aggressive sports during recess. This sometimes causes problems with the girls in her class, as they want to play jump rope and four square or house. However, when they talk to Saddie, they soon realize that she enjoys those activities as well.

Sarah and the girls' father, David Allen, divorced three years ago. David is a hard worker with a construction company of his own called Allen's Construction. He's a tall man, standing six feet, two inches. He has dark brown hair and a slender but muscular build. He is a kind, loving man who, unfortunately for those he loves, is a workaholic. The girls are supposed to have visits with their father several times a month; however, because of his work habits, they rarely see him.

***

Anna is getting frustrated with the image looking back at her in the large bathroom mirror. "Oh, why does there ever have to be such a thing as a bad hair day?"

she grumbles under her breath. Deciding to wet her hair down and start over, she kneels beside the oversized white porcelain bathtub and, after testing the warmth of the water, leans over the side, puts her head under the faucet, and lets the water fall over her head. After thoroughly rinsing her hair, she turns the water off, blindly reaches for the towel next to her, and wraps it around her head.

The sound of music echoes within the small space of this light lilac-colored room. The messier of the house's two bathrooms, it belongs entirely to Anna and Saddie. There is a vanity table positioned along one wall with a large mirror above it that has combs, brushes, and hair bands and ties strung all over it. Shampoo, conditioner and bath oil containers have also been placed haphazardly on the counter, the side of the tub, and in the cupboard.

After standing up, Anna begins to pat the excess water from her hair. As she turns on her hair dryer, she begins to sing to the music she's playing in the bathroom. Noticing that she can no longer hear the music, she turns it up over the sound of the dryer.

She has spent an hour getting ready for school, and it looks like she will spend another thirty minutes before she is ready. As she finishes with the blow dryer and turns it off, the loud music blares at Anna, making her jump. With a giggle, she reaches over and turns it down.

The curling iron has been on for a long time and of course is very hot, as Anna is about to find out. Holding up a gather of hair with her left hand and looking in the mirror instead of looking down at the iron, she accidentally grabs the wrong end of it with her right hand. Letting out a sharp "Yeouch!" she drops the iron and lets go of her hair. She takes a deep breath, picks up the iron, places it on the counter, and takes up her hair once again. This time she remembers which way the iron is facing and avoids being burned.

Anna is a very patient young woman; even when she is angry she is able to control herself. Anna's mom has taught her that it's normal and healthy to have feelings. She also taught her that the ways she expresses those emotions are just as important as having them. Most importantly, her mother has tried to teach Anna to be as understanding of herself as she is with others. So, although she has been burned and could have been angry with herself, Anna just shakes it off and goes back to what she was doing.

"Mom, have you seen my purple hair tie?" Anna shouts. Anna smiles wryly as she thinks to herself—*Oh, it's just one of those days when nothing seems to go right. You stub your toe getting out of bed, your favorite top has a big ol' stain on it from pizza sauce, the only pair of jeans that is clean has become too short, the only socks you find have a hole in the toe that bugs you half to death all day long, and to top it all off, it's Saturday and you didn't have to get out of bed at all.*

Sarah notices that Anna is wearing a purple T-shirt with sparkle lettering that reads "If you were me right now you'd be STUNNING!" and hip-hugger blue jeans that slightly flare out at the bottom and are a bit too long, so the hem is frayed from being walked on by her white and pink tennis shoes. Like most moms, Sarah has to keep an eye on what her daughters are wearing so that they don't wear a favorite pair of jeans three or four days in a row.

As most teenagers know, looking good is very important; however, looking your best comes with a price. That price is time, and with all the hairstyling, makeup, and clothes, Anna has almost run out of it this morning. Sarah has already given the last warning that they are leaving for school, and Anna decides to just put her hair up, and it is not going well. She is finally able to get it to look the way she wants it to, with most of it pulled back into a ponytail. Her bangs are curled under and lying just above her eyebrows, and long, curly strands frame her face.

Saddie is already in the car. Her morning has gone just the opposite of Anna's. She jumped out of bed, bathed, dressed, and ate breakfast all without a single problem. Unfortunately, that's all about to change. Saddie has been sitting patiently in the car for fifteen minutes, waiting for Anna and Sarah. Now her patience has worn out and she's honking the horn and yelling, "Hurry up!" *Honk! Honk!* Saddie begins to get frustrated.

"Let's go!" she yells from the car as it sits in the driveway. Sarah and Anna calmly get into the car with all of their umbrellas, purses, backpacks, jackets, and raincoats.

Finally in the car and backing out of the driveway, Sarah addresses Saddie and says, "Saddie, it is not polite to yell at people like that, or to hurry them along by honking the horn. It's rude."

"I know, Momma, but I'm supposed to talk to Julie before the bell rings this morning. And because of Miss Perfect, I won't have time now."

"Hey, watch it you little—" Anna says.

Sarah calmly interrupts by saying, "I know you're upset, but just because someone does something you don't like does not mean you have the right to be rude. This goes for the both of you." Sarah looks at Anna.

Soon the attitude in the car changes, and the three of them begin talking about the things they either want or need to do that day. Sarah begins with, "I work until two thirty, and I need to stop at the grocery store before coming home. That means it will be about three fifteen or three thirty by the time I get home. Do either of you have anything going on after school that I don't know about?"

"No," they say, responding at the same time.

"Julie and I are going to teach Misty a lesson about lying!" Saddie almost yells, wanting to make sure that she is next. "Misty has been lying a lot lately, and we're not going to put up with it anymore. So we're going to figure out a way to show her how it feels to be lied to."

"Did you tell Misty that you don't like it when she lies?" asks Anna.

"Well, no, that'd be rude! Besides, she should just know how it makes people feel in the first place," Saddie responds, irritated at Anna's question.

"Saddie," asked Sarah, "what if the girls in your class decided that you shouldn't be playing football with the boys. And instead of telling you how they felt, they decided to teach you a lesson by, oh, let's say, not talking to you until you stopped what you were doing. How would that make you feel?"

"First of all," Saddie said, "I'd be confused, because I wouldn't know why they stopped talking to me. Second, I'd be sad that they'd want me to stop being me. And third, I'd be mad, 'cause it isn't their job to tell me what I can and can't do." Suddenly, as though a light has turned on inside of Saddie's head, she realizes that what she and Julie were about to do to Misty was exactly what Sarah had just described.

"Oh!" Saddie exclaims, "I get it; we—or, I mean, I—need to talk to Misty and let her know how it makes me feel when she lies to me, and I should ask her to stop."

Sarah smiles and says, "Good job, Saddie; I'm proud of you for figuring that out."

"And if she doesn't stop, then we can teach her a lesson," Saddie says with a straight face.

"Saddie!" Sarah reprimands her.

"Just kidding," Saddie says with a laugh.

Before they know it, they're at Saddie's school. Sarah and Anna are trying to say their good-byes, but without saying a word, Saddie jumps out of the car and runs toward a girl with short, black hair: it's Julie. Sarah and Anna look at each other, shrug their shoulders, and smile. Saddie looks back and quickly waves as she realizes she forgot to say good-bye. Sarah and Anna both wave as they drive off.

Julie is dressed in jeans, a purple top under a pink raincoat, and tennis shoes. She has been standing in the drizzle, leaning against the side of the building with her right leg bent and her foot against the wall while she stood on her left leg, waiting for Saddie. When she sees Saddie, she instantly leans forward and runs to meet her. The girls have five minutes before the bell rings, and they plan to make each second of them count. At first Julie is disappointed that they are not going to be teaching Misty a lesson, but after listening to Saddie explain why it would not be a good idea, she feels better and decides to join Saddie in caringly confronting Misty.

***

Anna and Sarah talk during the rest of the drive to Anna's school, Eastern Junior High. With concern, Anna says, "Mom, I need to ask you a question."

"Yes, Anna, what is it?" Sarah asks.

"You remember my friend Christina? Well, I'm worried about her. She seems so sad lately, and I don't know why, or what I should do. What do you think I should do?" Anna asks very seriously.

"What do you think you can do?" Sarah asks softly.

"I don't know. I mean, we haven't been very close lately. We've just drifted apart, or I would just ask her," Anna responds sadly.

"What do you mean drifted apart?" Sarah asks.

"Well, I guess it's been about three months now since we've talked. It started out when she'd only say a few words, like when I'd ask her how she was doing and she would say, 'I'm fine,' 'I'm okay, I guess,' and 'Pretty good.' Then she started avoiding me altogether. I'd see her coming down the hall, and she'd look away and not answer me when I would say hello or call her by name. She has her head down all the time, never making eye contact with anyone—friends, classmates, or teachers. I didn't know what to do; talking to her seemed to only upset her. So I just started leaving her alone, and it appears as though everyone else is doing the same. It's gone on for too long, and I'm starting to get worried about her."

"Anna, you and Christina have been friends since the first day of kindergarten. I bet if you sat her down and confronted her, you'd be able to find out what's bothering her. What do you think?"

After a few seconds of silence, Anna declares, "You know what, I bet I could!"

Usually, Anna would not have hugged her mother when she was dropped off at school—it's embarrassing for anyone to think that you're still a baby and that you need a hug from your mommy—but today she gives her mother a big hug and says, "Thanks, Mom! I love you!" *Sometimes Mom knows just what to do,* Anna thinks to herself as she waves good-bye.

Chapter 2

Meeting Christina

Anna has decided to try to talk to Christina during lunch. This makes the morning pass slowly, as she finds herself not being able to concentrate. Staring out the window, Anna is so deep in thought she doesn't notice that the sound of her teacher's voice has been drowned out by the sound of rain on the windows. And as everyone knows, as soon as you stop paying attention, that's when you're asked a question.

"Miss Allen, what is the answer to number twelve? Miss Allen? *Miss Allen?*" Mr. Janus, the fourth period math teacher, is clearly upset.

Because of his full head of chocolate brown hair, brown eyes, clean-shaven face, and handsome features, many of the girls in the class have had a crush on Mr. Janus at one time or another. Their crushes don't last long, though, as they find out that Mr. Janus has a Napoleon complex due to his five feet, six inches, and his being shorter than many of his students. He feels that his stature is the reason the students sometimes do not listen to him. In other words, he takes their normal teenage daydreaming personally. So he asks Anna this question on purpose, partially to make her pay attention and partially to get even with her for disrespecting him.

Embarrassed but confident, Anna says, "Huh, what problem?"

"You really need to pay attention, Anna. That was number twelve," Mr. Janus says, trying to shame her.

"Oh, fifty-three is the answer to number twelve," Anna quickly answers.

"Tha—tha—that's correct," Mr. Janus says, stuttering out his surprise at her not even having to look at her paper for the answer. He decides not to ask her any more questions to avoid being embarrassed again.

Anna immediately starts to worry about Christina again. As much as she wants to help Christina, she doesn't want to lose her friend, and yet not doing anything is causing her friendship to slowly slip away.

While thinking about Christina, Anna remembers that Christina was once considered one of the most popular girls in school. Because of her combination of cuteness and contagious laughter that showed off her sense of humor, she used to be admired by everyone. Christina is also one of the top students in her class, receiving straight As. Anna remembers a conversation she had with her friends Katie and Nichoal about Christina.

"I tried to talk to Christina the other day: no luck, dude. She told me that I wouldn't understand, whatever that means," Katie said.

"Yeah, and I waved at her and she totally blew me off. I know she saw me; she looked right at me. What's up with that?" Nichoal said.

"Christina has been shutting everyone out," Anna agreed. "Have you noticed—even the teachers aren't doing anything?"

"It's because her grades are still top of the class—", Katie said, "and they don't mess with people who get good grades."

Nichoal said, "And what's up with her new look? I mean really, is it punk, gothic, skater, or total rebellion? Geez, pick one will ya—oh and I don't think she's bathing either."

Christina has begun wearing very baggy clothes that seem related to her new attitude. These include bland, plain T-shirts that are three or four times too big for her. And she usually wears a very large, stained, solid black-hooded sweatshirt that hangs down almost to her knees, with the hood up and pulled down over her face. Sometimes she wears a dull gray coat that makes her look like a six-year-old who's wearing her father's coat. The sleeves hang five or six inches past her fingertips, and the bottom of it goes past her knees. Her shoulder-length black hair had always been groomed perfectly and was never out of place, but now it is stringy and greasy, and it looks as though it has not been washed for weeks. It hangs in her face, hiding the fact that she has quit using lip gloss and the little bit of makeup that had previously been so carefully applied. Faded blue jeans two sizes too large hang on her over an old pair of dirty sneakers. Anna knows it isn't just a phase, but that something is bothering her friend. Christina seemed her normal self just fourteen weeks earlier, and now she is someone who Anna doesn't recognize. Something is wrong, horribly wrong!

Quick glances at the clock reveal that even as slow

as time seems to be moving, lunchtime is approaching, and Anna begins to become more and more nervous. She takes a deep breath and resigns herself to the fact that Christina needs her. As she begins to look out the window again, Anna says to herself, *I'm going to help her whether Christina likes it or not. Besides, what do I have to lose? Christina and I haven't been close for a few months now; if that doesn't change, at least I'll know I have tried everything.*

When the bell rings, it startles Anna so much that she almost jumps out of her seat. Her arm sends her math book to the floor with a loud slap. Everyone looks in the direction of the noise to see what has happened. They see Anna pick up her book and quickly leave the classroom. Anna's two friends Katie and Nichoal look at each other.

Katie says, "I wonder what's up with her? She's been acting strange all day," Nichoal just shrugs her shoulders. Out in the hallway, Anna nervously makes her way through the crowd of people heading to the cafeteria.

Even though she has lost her appetite, Anna navigates the lunch line and puts some food on her plate, thinking that playing with it might give her something to do if she becomes more nervous. She looks once again for Christina. The cafeteria is unusually crowded because of the rainy weather. Even with the many people that are moving around and talking, it doesn't take her long to find Christina in her usual place. A table in the corner of the cafeteria, away from windows and the rest of the student population, has become Christina's sanctuary at school. She is alone, which makes Anna feel sad and grateful at the same time. She feels sad because nobody seems to care and grateful because this way their conversation won't be interrupted.

Anna slowly picks her way through the crowd, waving to friends along the way. She smiles and shakes her head as her friend Katie insistently tries to wave her over. Still trying to plot a course through the hordes of people, she briefly says hello to those that greet her. Anna is trying to be nice but is becoming frustrated. *I hope I make it before she leaves!* Anna thinks worriedly. As she approaches, Anna notices that even though Christina's back is against the wall, she doesn't react to Anna's approach. The way she is staring into her tray of uneaten food makes her look as if she is dead or frozen stiff.

"Hi Christina!" Anna says, falsely cheerful.

Christina jumps as though a gun was fired next to her ear. "Huh!" she screams. "Oh, it's you," she says, barely mumbling loudly enough for Anna to hear. Anna notices that when her eyes meet Christina's, she sees a look of horror staring back at her, and Christina is trembling so badly that she almost drops her fork.

"Oh, sweetie, I didn't mean to scare you!" Anna says apologetically. "We haven't talked for a long time, and I was wondering how you're doing."

"I'm fine!" Christina replies coldly.

"Is this seat taken?" asks Anna.

"No, but I don't want to—," Christina says, whispering. But it was too late; Anna sat down before Christina could finish.

The question of whether or not Christina had been bathing is very quickly answered as a foul smell crosses under Anna's nose. Concerned that the crowd in the cafeteria is so loud that she might have to yell at Christina and that she might loose her appetite from the odor of what must have been weeks of not bathing, Anna decides to play with her food for a while.

When she finally breaks the awkward silence and asks, "Christina, do you remember all the fun times we have had?" she is surprised that Christina can hear her. Even more surprising is that, as Christina continues to look blankly into her tray of food, Anna hears her whisper, "Yes."

Anna notices that Christina is getting restless, so she

quickly forces herself to begin to giggle and says, "How about the Princess Poo-Poo Head incident?" Christina tries very hard to conceal a smile, but her dull grey eyes sparkle and give her away.

It is the first time that Anna has seen any emotion in Christina for a long time. Even when everyone in the class was laughing, Christina never showed any inkling of being happy. Anna thinks herself, *This is a sign that maybe, just maybe, I can get her to open up.*

Christina looks up at her and slightly grins. Anna asks, "Do you remember how old we were?"

"Not really," Christina answers.

"I think we were eight years old, and that would have made Saddie, um, four. Yeah, that would be about right. You had come over to spend the night as you used to do so often back then, and we had been excluding Saddie from playing with us, again. The next thing we knew, she had come down the stairs. Do you remember what she looked like, with her Wonder Girl underwear on her head?"

"And her pony tails sticking out the leg holes!" Christina adds.

Anna stumbles through the rest of the story, pausing often because she is laughing so hard. "She was wearing mom's pink robe with the arms rolled up.... It was so big that it flowed behind her like a royal train." Anna lets out a snicker. "The toilet plunger in her hand, held up like a scepter, saying, 'I'm a princess.'" Anna is giggling so hard now she has to stop telling the story. Christina's grin slowly begins to turn into a smile. She catches herself softly chuckling and tries to stop, but as Anna's laughter continues, she is no longer able to contain herself and begins to laugh out loud.

Christina stops laughing long enough to say, "And you said, 'Princess! Yeah, Princess Poo-Poo Head!' and we began laughing so hard we both thought we would wet our pants. Your mom came in to see what was going on, and we introduced Saddie to her: 'Now introducing … Her Highness … Princess Poo-Poo Head!'" Christina erupts in laughter.

"And—and—your mom started giggling, trying not to upset Saddie, but couldn't help herself."

Then Anna chimes in, saying, "and Saddie just loved it and was beaming because she was getting all of this attention, and she tried to knight us all with her plunger scepter—but—we all ran away because we didn't want to be touched by it. So Mom went into the kitchen and came back with a long-handled wooden spoon, and one at a time we all knelt down and became the Knightesses of Princess Poo-Poo Head's Court."

The two girls laugh and giggle for several minutes, remembering the scene. Then Christina stops and looks at Anna and says, "Oh, Anna, I've missed you so much. I'm so lost and miserable." The laughter of a few moments ago abruptly turns into tears. While crying herself, Anna wraps her arms around Christina. The girls bury their heads into each other's shoulders and weep.

Neither girl feels that the tears will ever end. Anna rubs and pats Christina's back through her oversized coat and sweatshirt, trying to calm her. When Christina finally does quit crying, both of the girls become aware that they are alone in the cafeteria. Everyone else has left.

"How long have we been here?" Anna wonders out loud. The clock on the wall answers her question, and she realizes that they are ten minutes late for fifth period. Christina starts to get up, but Anna asks her to stay and talk. She hesitantly sits down. Anna reaches out and pushes the dirty, grimy hood back and brushes the greasy, unkempt hair out of Christina's eyes and says, "there you are!" Embarrassed, Christina looks away.

"Christina what's happened to you?" Anna asks. "Why've you pushed everyone away?"

Chapter 3

Dreaded Information

"You've got to promise not to tell anyone. Do you promise?" Christina warily asks. Anna doesn't say anything for a while. She is mentally transported back to a conversation that she and Sarah had had when she was younger than Saddie is now, which would have made her about six or seven. It had been one of the earlier conversations that Sarah would have with Anna about the "birds and the bees." This particular conversation was about how no one had the right to touch Anna in any way that did not feel comfortable to her. If they did not listen to her *No!* and touched her anyway, she needed to tell someone right away. Sarah had told her, "Sometimes people do things that they are not supposed to, and they will try to get you to promise not to tell."

"That's a secret, right Mommy?" Anna blurted out.

"That's right, honey, a very bad secret, and keeping those kinds of secrets hurts not only us, but possibly others, so it is very important not to keep bad secrets, okay?"

"Okay, Mommy, but how can it hurt other people if I keep a secret?" Anna asked.

"Say that someone at school who is bigger and maybe older than you started picking on you, hitting you, and pushing you around, and they told you not to tell anyone or they would hurt you. Then they started hurting other children and doing the same thing to them. Now, because of not telling anyone, many people are being hurt. Understand?"

"Oh, so if I keep a bad secret for someone, they might

hurt someone else and make them keep a bad secret too, and the bad just keeps growing bigger and bigger," said Anna.

"That's right!" Sarah said.

"I promise to never keep bad secrets" Anna stated, very proud of herself.

"Christina," Anna finally responds. "I really think it would help you to tell me what's happening to you, but I can't keep a secret if it means you're in danger. It'd make me responsible if you or someone else continues to be hurt. And I'm not going to lie to you and say that I'll keep a secret when I know that if it is hurtful, I'm not going to."

"You don't understand; if I tell, he'll kill you," says Christina.

"Who'll kill me, Christina?" Anna fearfully asks.

"I just don't know if I can say it out loud," Christina

whispers.

There is a horrible silence that fills the cafeteria for a few moments as Christina thinks about what Anna said. Christina thinks to herself, *I've got to do something; I can't keep living like this! Anna is my friend, and I trust her. I have to tell; I have to tell someone.*

Christina finds herself talking before she realizes that words are coming out of her mouth. "My brother James has been coming into my room at night and making me do things with him. It's horrible. I pretend to be asleep every time, but that doesn't stop him. He makes sure that I'm awake by pushing me, or if I pretend too long, he hits me. He touches me in my private parts and makes me touch his." She shudders and says, "It makes my skin crawl just thinking about it. When he's done, I curl up under the blankets and cry myself to sleep. Before he leaves my room, he always says, 'This was your fault; you made me want to do this. If you tell anyone, I will kill them. I don't care who it is; I will kill them, and it will be your fault!'"

Christina talks without tears, her voice quiet but clear like ice. "That's why I've never told you. I had to avoid you; I knew I couldn't talk to you without telling you. I needed you to be safe." After a short pause, Christina continues. "I've tried to tell my mother so many times, but I just keep chickening out. James is the one that everyone looks up to. It'd crush them if they knew … if … if they even believed me. I don't know what I would do if I told them and they didn't believe me, and—oh my God—then to have James follow through with what he promised. I couldn't; I wouldn't be able to live with it. So I can't eat; my stomach is always tied in knots. I don't sleep, afraid that he will be there, and I don't talk to anyone except when I have to. I don't shower, hoping that if I stink he'll leave me alone. It doesn't help, but I keep doing it anyway." Christina stops and looks at Anna, expecting to see a look of disgust or contempt on her face. Instead, she sees a look of compassion, and empathy as tears are running down her cheeks.

Anna takes Christina into her arms and says, "You are so strong to survive what's happening to you and to overcome your fears by telling me about the horrors he's put you through." With that, both girls begin to cry. They hold each other very tightly, to the point that it begins to become uncomfortable, but neither loosens her grip on the other.

After what seems like an eternity, Christina pulls away and says, "And you know what the worst part is?"

"No, what?" asks Anna.

"A part of me likes it," Christina says with her head hanging down. "I like that James wants to spend time with me. He's never been interested in me before, and this is something we have together. And sometimes it even feels good. I feel so dirty and disgusting; I wish I were dead!" Christina begins to sob uncontrollably again.

As Anna holds Christina, she remembers another conversation that she and Sarah had. She was older this time; in fact it was just two years ago, when Anna started her period and was developing breasts. Sarah and Anna were sitting at the white kitchen table; Anna's feet barely touched the floor when she sat all the way back in her chair.

"Now that you are changing into a young woman," Sarah said, "the boys in school will be curious about what is going on with you. They may try to touch you, and if they do, you need to tell them to keep their hands to themselves and tell someone about it."

"Like a bad secret?" Anna asks.

"Yes, just like a bad secret," Sarah replies. "I want you to understand, Anna, that you might like the attention, and you might even find pleasure in having someone touch you, but if it feels strange and uncomfortable, you have the right to say no, and you need to tell someone.

What those individuals are doing is wrong and against the law; they do not have the right to touch someone without that person's permission." Sarah talked to Anna like she was more grown-up than ever before, which made her pay attention to what Sarah was saying.

"If I don't want to be touched," Anna asked, "then how can it still feel good?"

Sarah thought for a moment and said, "God made us so that sexual contact between people feels good so that we want to have sex to create new life."

"Babies!?" Anna shouted, excited that she had figured it out herself.

"Yes, babies." Sarah said, smiling. "If people didn't feel good while having sex, then they'd never do it, and then there'd never be any babies."

"Oh!" Anna replied while trying to apply what she understood as feeling good to the pictures of reproduction

Sarah had painted during past conversations.

Sarah, noticing that Anna was struggling, decided to try to give another explanation.

"Anna," Sarah asked. "When you get tickled, does it feel good?"

"Yes," Anna replied.

"That is kind of what it's like with sex; it's a physical feeling of pleasure. But when you are tickled and don't want to be tickled, how does that feel?" Sarah asked.

"It starts making me mad because I didn't want to be tickled and I can't stop it," Anna said.

"Do you still laugh even though you didn't want to be tickled?" Sarah continued.

Anna nodded her head. "Yes," she answered.

"That is what it's like with unwanted sexual contact. You see, even if you don't want to be tickled, it still feels good and makes you laugh. That leads to feelings of anger at ourselves for not being able to control what has just happened to us and for feeling pleasure from something we think we shouldn't find pleasurable. Understand, honey?"

"Yes, I think so," Anna replied, feeling pleased with herself.

Having a better understanding of why Christina is feeling the way she is, Anna tries to console her friend. "Christina, I'm always going to be here for you, no matter what. Now, if you're ready, we'd better get to class."

"I suppose," Christina responds. "I know you said that you couldn't promise not to tell, Anna, but, I really wish … um, that … ah … well, you know, that you wouldn't—for your sake. I mean, I'm not sure if James meant what he said or not, and I don't want anything to happen to you. I … I need you." With that, Christina, not waiting for a response from her dear friend, turns and quickly walks out of the cafeteria and doesn't look back.

As soon as Christina is out of sight, Anna begins to cry. She lets out all of the emotions that she has been holding back while talking to Christina. She wants to help her friend rather than be supported by her. All the sadness and sheer rage at James's disgusting behavior toward her beloved friend comes out painfully. Like an ever increasing tide, each sob brings more tears and louder sobs until she lets out a scream that echoes through the now empty cafeteria: *why!* Making a decision to talk to someone and letting it all out somehow helps Anna feel a little better about things. Once she has begun to calm down, Anna gathers up and puts away both her and Christina's lunch trays and makes her way out of the cafeteria.

Chapter 4

Breaking the Silence

Anna finds herself sitting outside the school counselor's office, needing to talk to someone. She just can't wait until she sees Sarah again. She has to tell someone; this is too much to carry. Anna decides that since she has missed most of her fifth period anyway and needs to go to the office to get a pass, she will try to visit with the school counselor, Mrs. Davis.

The chair in front and to the right of the school secretary's desk is comfortable, but not comfortable enough for Anna to forget why she is there. To the left of the secretary's desk is a door with a sign above it that reads "Principal." To the right of the desk is another door with a large tinted window with white lettering that reads, "Counselor." It is quiet at the moment, the only sound being the *tap, tap, tap* of computer keys the secretary presses as she types a letter. This quiet only gives Anna time to reflect on all the things that Christina has told her. This will soon change when the bell for sixth period rings, letting out all the other students. While waiting for Mrs. Davis, images of Christina's brother flash in and out of Anna's mind, and she has a hard time imagining this blond-haired, blue-eyed, charismatic person as a rapist. But she believes Christina and will support her with everything she has. *That jerk*, Anna thinks to herself.

"Miss Allen, I can see you now," a meek little voice says from the doorway. Mrs. Davis, a frail-looking, slender woman who stands only four feet, ten inches tall with strawberry blonde hair and sharp green eyes, has a reputation of being blunt with her students. Being shorter than average for a grown woman and petite, she looks very young for her age, which occasionally leads to her being mistaken for a student, especially by the new students at the beginning of each year. Because of this, she wears business-style pantsuits to give her the appearance of authority. Today she is wearing a mint green suit, matching high heels to give her more status, and a cream-colored blouse.

"Please have a seat," Mrs. Davis softly says. Anna takes a seat in one of the two unpadded wooden armchairs sitting next to each other in front of a large mahogany-colored desk. The room is brightly painted in rich yellows, peaches, and lavenders. Several large windows along the south wall and two large bay windows, which make up the entire west wall, illuminate the room. Anna smiles as she thinks to herself, *every time I come in here and look at all of these plants, I remember why the other students call this the Psycho-Jungle.* There are various plants, ferns and ivies sitting on the long bookshelf along the east wall by the door. Small African violets in decorative pots reside on all four corners of her desk. Several different species of peacock plants, whose leaves resemble the beautiful feathers of its namesake, live on stands and shelves behind the desk along the south wall.

A large rubber plant that resembles a tree stands at the corner of the south and west walls and stretches over six feet tall. Many variations of hanging plants—such as Achimenes, with its pretty, tubular flowers, and many different types of ivy—impair the view out the west window.

The north wall is also home to plants of different sizes, shapes, and colors. These sit on tiers of plant stands of differing sizes and heights. Together they provide the appearance of a cascade of foliage. Many of the plant's soils need to be watered on a daily basis, which makes the office very humid, even in the cool October weather.

Anna notices that Mrs. Davis has many books that are partially hidden by the plants—all ninety-eight of them. The subjects of these books include topics such as child development, adolescent psychology, career counseling, anger management, and many others.

"What can I do for you, Anna?" Mrs. Davis asks in a girlish tone.

"Mrs. Davis I … I … I don't know where to start." Anna replies.

"Well, why not start from the beginning, honey," Mrs. Davis says. She is always calling people honey, sweetie, dear, and pumpkin in a nauseatingly sweet, girlish way that is very snooty, and it causes many students to seek out someone else to talk to when they are having problems.

Anna takes a deep breath and begins to tell Mrs. Davis everything about her conversation with Christina, even the Princess Poo-Poo Head story. While she is telling Mrs. Davis what has happened, Anna tries to get a sense of how Mrs. Davis is reacting to what she is describing. At one point Mrs. Davis gets up from her desk, grabs a spray bottle full of water and begins gently misting the plants on the south wall, turning her back to Anna.

"Go ahead dear, I can still hear you," Mrs. Davis says, reassuring Anna as she notices an irritation in Anna's voice.

Anna doesn't get the response she is hoping for when she finishes. Instead of understanding the pain that Christina is suffering from and Anna's concern, Mrs. Davis turns from watering her plants, looks right at Anna, and says in her childlike voice, "I know James, and he would never do anything like that. He is a very nice boy. I think Christina is jealous of her brother and is looking for attention. She developed this whopper to get attention from others, and that's why she's altering her appearance. She didn't come with you today to tell me because she knows that I, as a trained professional, will see through her façade. My suggestion is that she grows up and stops blaming others for her lack of abilities."

"I have never seen anyone as insensitive in my life as

you are being right now. How dare you judge Christina when you don't even know her! If you knew her, you would see how much she is suffering, and until today, when I *forced* her to talk to me, she was suffering in complete silence and isolation. You call yourself a counselor? Hah! You're a joke." With that, she turns and walks out of Mrs. Davis's office. Mrs. Davis just shrugs her shoulders and turns back to caring for her many plants.

"She will see that I'm right," Mrs. Davis says to her plants. "I'm always right; isn't that so, my little darlings? Momma is always right!" Anna is so angry when she leaves Mrs. Davis's office that she starts crying on her way back to class, which makes her even angrier. She decides to go to the restroom and freshen up before going to class. She doesn't want to have to explain to the teacher why she has been crying.

By the time she reaches class, Anna is not interested in listening to her teacher, being in class, or even in being in school. She is thinking about what she needs to do next to help Christina. *If Mrs. Davis reacted this way and she is supposed to be a professional, how will others respond? What will Mom think? Who should I talk to? Should I tell anyone? Yes, I have to tell someone. Mom will know what to do, I hope! It's no wonder Christina didn't want to say anything!* Because Anna is asking herself all these questions, she isn't noticing that time is getting away from her, and she jumps when the final bell of the day rings.

As Anna thinks about Christina, the bus ride to her usual drop-off point is one of reflection and worry. She meets Saddie there as usual so that the two can walk home together. Walking on the narrow sidewalk positioned in front of modest yet attractive middle-class homes, Saddie notices that her sister is unusually quiet and asks, "Is something wrong, Anna?"

"I'm worried about Christina," Anna says.

"Why?" Saddie asks.

"Someone has been hurting her," Anna replies.

"Who?" Saddie asks.

"None of your business," Anna says.

"Fine, but you have to tell an adult, Anna; that's what Mom says," Saddie says a bit bossily.

"I know, Saddie. I did tell an adult already, but it didn't do any good." Anna rolls her eyes as she recalls the session in the Psycho-Jungle. "Now I'm worried about telling another adult and getting the same response."

"Mom won't be like that!" Saddie exclaims, agitated.

"I know," Anna says. The two girls walk the rest of the way home without saying a word; Anna is lost in thought about her friend and how Sarah will react to the news and Saddie is irritated at Anna for not trusting their mother in the first place.

Chapter 5

Mother's Help

"I don't know what to do," Anna says to her mother. "I mean, I've already talked to an adult, and she didn't help a bit. What would that have done to Christina if she'd been the one to talk to Mrs. Davis? Will everyone I talk to be the same way? If so, then what's the point?"

"You didn't get that response from me," Sarah says.

"But you're different; you're my mom," Anna says.

"I could've blamed Christina for what happened to her, just as easily as Mrs. Davis did. But I didn't, and neither will others, Anna. There are two things that we need to do right now. First, we need to call the National

Child Abuse Hotline at 1-800-4achild and tell that person what Christina told you. Second, we need to talk to a person at our local Department of Health and Human Services (DHHS)."

"But what if they don't believe me? What if they show up at Christina's house and start asking a bunch of questions and leave her there to get into trouble? What if—"

"What happens if we don't do anything, Anna?"

Anna suddenly stops. "Then James continues to hurt her, and possibly others," Anna says.

"That's right, honey, and we don't want that," Sarah calmly responds. "You have to trust me when I say that the people at DHHS are trained professionals that will know exactly what to do and can answer all of your questions."

Since it is already four thirty and Sarah knows that

Child Protective Service (CPS) workers get off work at five, they decide to call their local DHHS office first. Sarah talks to a woman named Valerie who sets up an appointment for both Sarah and Anna to come into the office the next day at one o'clock.

After talking to Valerie, Sarah looks at Anna and says, "It's time to call the hotline and let them know what happened today." Sarah places the phone on the large, cherry dining room table between herself and Anna.

"I'm going to put the phone on speaker in case you need me," Sarah says. "Ready?"

"As much as I ever will be," Anna says. As Sarah dials the phone, Anna can feel her heart start to race and a lump begin to rise in her throat.

A calm, pleasant voice on the other end says, "Child Protective Services, this is Nancy, how can I help you today?" The calmness of Nancy's voice helps slightly to ease Anna's nerves.

"Hi, my name is Sarah Allen. My daughter, Anna Allen, and I would like to report the abuse of Anna's friend Christina. We are both here on speakerphone."

Nancy, still in her calm, pleasant voice says, "Okay, Sarah, first I need to ask you a few questions, and you need to know that we are going to record this conversation for accuracy of information. Everything you say will be kept strictly confidential, and your names will not be shared with anyone but our staff, okay?"

"Okay," Sarah says.

Then Nancy asks for Sarah's full name, address, and phone number. She also asks for Christina's full name, age, and address. As Sarah begins to give Nancy this information, a sudden fear comes over Anna. Her heart races, and the palms of her hands begin to sweat. *There's no turning back now,* she realizes. *I hope I'm doing the right thing for Christina*

"Anna?" Nancy asks.

"Yes?"

"Could you please give me your full name, age, and address?"

"Anna Kathleen Allen. I'm thirteen years old and live at 456 South D Street, Ord, Nebraska, 69875," Anna says meekly, as her nerves are still on edge. Nancy then asks Anna to tell her about Christina's abuse. Anna isn't sure where to start, so she begins with the conversation she had with Sarah that morning, on the way to school.

Anna is able to get through her entire story without breaking down emotionally. In fact, the more she talks, the angrier she becomes. Sarah touches Anna's shoulder to reassure her, and this helps Anna to calm down.

Nancy, still in her supportive voice says, "Anna, Sarah, I will submit this information to our team and they will look at everything you've told me and then make a decision about whether or not to investigate. Please understand, the decision to investigate is about determining the level of danger that Christina is in, not about determining whether or not you've told me the truth. You will receive a letter in the mail explaining whether an investigation will occur or not. If they decide not to investigate, they will give you a brief explanation as to why. Do you have any questions at this time?"

"No," Sarah and Anna say, at the same time.

"Thank you both very much for caring enough to report abuse," Nancy says. "Take care."

"Good-bye," they all say at once.

Anna takes a deep breath and slowly lets it out. Sarah looks at her and asks, "Are you okay, honey?"

She folds her arms on the table, lays her head down on them, and begins to weep. Sarah scoots her chair around the side of the table so that she is sitting next to Anna. She puts her arm across Anna's shoulders and rubs her arm.

"It's going to be okay, Anna. Christina is a strong person, and with the right help she is going to be fine." At this, Anna begins to cry harder, letting out all of the pent-up emotions from the day.

Between sobs, Anna finally is able to get out a few words. "I just feel so bad for Christina, and I hate the thought of her being in the same house as James."

"I understand, honey," Sarah says consolingly.

Just then both Sarah and Anna hear a noise coming from behind the door that leads from the kitchen to the dining room. It sounds to them like someone crying; they hear whimpering and sniffling.

"Saddie? Have you been listening in this whole time?" Sarah questioningly and soothingly calls out.

"Yes," Saddie meekly says with a sniffle.

"Come here, then," Sarah calls out. Saddie emerges from behind the door and slowly and sheepishly walks toward Sarah. When she gets close enough, Sarah reaches out her arms, and Saddie lunges into her mother's lap. Sarah holds Saddie close to her and asks, "Are you okay?" Saddie nods her head. Sarah then asks, "Do you have any questions about what you heard?"

Saddie hesitates, then asks, "What's going to happen now, I mean to Christina and James?"

"Well, hopefully Christina will stop being hurt, get the help she needs, and start to feel better about herself," Sarah says. "As for James, I'm not sure. He might go to jail, or he might go to a place where he can get some help. Hopefully he will realize that what he has done is harmful. And then again, he might not ever accept it. Either way, the main thing is that we've stopped the cycle and helped Christina."

Recognizing that Saddie understands the situation with Christina, Sarah decides to the change the subject and asks, "So, how did your meeting with Julie and Misty go today?"

"Oh, I don't know," Saddie says, mumbling. Seeing the questioning look on Sarah's face, she continues, saying, "Well, Julie and I did what you said for us to do, and Misty seemed to understand how we felt."

"But …" Sarah says encouragingly.

"But I feel she's still lying to us."

"Do you think that feeling might be because you just don't trust her?" asks Sarah.

Saddie thinks for a few minutes and then says, "That's a part of it, but I think it's more than that. I just don't know what it is … yet." Sarah decides to drop the conversation. She knows that sooner or later Saddie is going to figure out what is going on with Misty.

After all the stress and excitement of the afternoon, everyone is hungry. Sarah, also feeling tired from the afternoon's events, does not feel like fixing anything for supper and says, "How about pizza tonight, guys?" Both Anna and Saddie excitedly agree as Sarah reaches for the phone.

Chapter 6

Waiting for Answers

Would Christina refuse to tell the investigators what has happened to her? Would she be mad at Anna? What would James do? How would Christina's family react? Would they support Christina or James? Could they support both at the same time? What did Christina have to endure? These questions kept Anna tossing and turning most of the night. She just couldn't sleep while worrying about Christina.

Even though she is awake, the alarm clock startles Anna as it sounds off. She gets out of bed and leaves on her pajamas—which consist of one of Dad's old blue T-shirts and pink sweatpants that have been cut off just above the knee—puts her purple robe on, and wanders downstairs for breakfast. Mom is already up, but still wears her red nightshirt and blue full-length robe, and she has made pancakes, eggs, sausage, and toast. Also, pitchers of milk and orange juice have been set out on the table. The table has been set with love, and the food looks delicious. With a droopy-eyed smile, Anna says, "Looks like you couldn't sleep either."

"You're right," Sarah says, smiling at Anna.

Even though Anna doesn't have much of an appetite, she places one of each item on her plate and pours herself a glass of milk and a glass of orange juice. Everything looks very good, and she knows how hard her mom has worked. She doesn't want to be rude.

Just then, Saddie comes bounding into the dinning room. She also is still wearing her pajamas, but hers consist of a long-sleeved white shirt depicting brown ponies whose long, tan manes and tails are blowing in the wind, and white pants with brown cuffs at the ankles. Saddie, unlike her mother and sister, refuses to wear a robe. Instead, she likes to wear a pink sweater that is two sizes too big. It has a hole in the right sleeve between her wrist and elbow and a torn left pocket. She loves this sweater so much that she tried to wear it to school once, but Sarah firmly told her no.

As she sees all of the food on the table, she blurts out, "Who died?"

"Saddie!" Sarah shouts.

"That's not very nice." Anna adds.

"Well, we never get this kind of breakfast unless it's Sunday and we have company," Saddie explains. "I figured something bad had to happen to get all of this on a school day."

Sarah says, "You're right to be surprised, Saddie; this isn't normal for us. I had a hard time sleeping last night and woke early and thought I would fix us all a nice breakfast. Is that okay?"

"Oh, yes, it's wonderful!" Saddie exclaims.

Sarah notices that Anna has been lost in thought all during breakfast. She asks her, "Anna, will you be able to concentrate at school this morning? Would it be better for you to stay at home?"

"I don't know. All I can think about is Christina. I think if I go to class, maybe I can think about something else. But I'm afraid that's not what's going to happen."

"I think you're right, sweetie; you're not going to be able to concentrate on anything but Christina for a while," Sarah says soothingly. "I'd feel better if you stayed home today."

"Okay, but I'm not looking forward to waiting until one o'clock to talk to someone from CPS. It doesn't matter whether I'm at home or at school."

"I want to stay home too," Saddie jumps in. "I'm upset about what is going on, and I'm not sure I can concentrate on anything either."

Sarah smiles, knowing full well that Saddie is acting, and just wants to stay home from school. Sarah also knows that although Saddie has her parts of the fall concert memorized, she is looking forward to rehearsal, and so she says, "I thought you were supposed to have rehearsal for your concert today? Are you sure you want to skip it? Won't everyone miss you?"

Saddie's eyes nearly jump out of their sockets with surprise, and she says, "Oh! I forgot! I can't miss it!" She gathers herself and reluctantly adds, "Um, I guess I'll be fine. It'll be hard, but I'll just have to think about the concert."

"That's awfully brave of you, Saddie. I wish I were as strong as you," Anna says with a supportive smile. With that, Saddie beams with self-satisfaction, and after consuming two eggs, one pancake, four pieces of bacon, one glass of orange juice, and one glass of milk, she excuses herself from the table. After politely leaving the dining room, she bolts up to her room and happily picks out her clothes for the day.

While Sarah is taking Saddie to school, Anna decides to shower and get dressed. The process is much simpler today than yesterday. She showers and washes her hair. Instead of taking the time to style her hair, she decides to comb it out, fluff it up with her fingers, and let it dry on its own. She looks in her closet but just cannot figure out what she wants to wear. She finally picks out a light lavender–colored T-shirt that has dark lavender stitching around the seams, and a white hooded sweatshirt. She rifles through her dresser drawers and chooses a pair of bright-pink sweatpants. She pulls the legs of them up almost to her knees so they look more like capri pants. She finishes her look with lavender-striped socks and white tennis shoes.

Anna struggles to keep from thinking about Christina and the appointment with DHHS. She turns on the TV and surfs through the channels. This helps for a while, until it seems that every show has something to do with a girl or woman being abused. Anna tries to read a book about horses but cannot concentrate. Sarah comes home and keeps herself busy with household chores, and Anna asks to help.

"Sure," Sarah says, after noticing that Anna is desperately looking for something to keep herself busy. "Why don't you go gather up all of you and your sister's dirty clothes and meet me at the washer?"

"Okay," Anna says rather reluctantly. "I want something to do, but touching Saddie's dirty clothes isn't what I had in mind."

Suddenly, Anna discovers that it is eleven o'clock and that she is actually hungry. "Wow, I can't believe how fast time has gone," Anna says to Sarah.

"I know; it's amazing not only how much a person can accomplish, but also how fast time can go when you keep busy," Sarah says happily. "We had better get ready if we're going to eat something before we go to our appointment."

They both look into the mirror to make sure that they are presentable before leaving. The sun is shining brightly and enables the fall colors to jump out. Anna puts on her white hoodie, expecting it to be chilly outside. To her delight, the sunshine has warmed things up to a nice fall sixty-five degrees. With the grey, dark, clouds and rain of yesterday gone and replaced by sunshine and warmth, Anna feels confident that things are going to be okay.

Chapter 7

Helping Heroes

Anna finds herself sitting on a hard, uncomfortable wooden chair. There are several of these in a row against the wall. The walls of the room are painted white and hold several pictures, posters, and paintings. Many have sayings like "If at first you don't succeed, you must be doing something wrong; try doing it differently." The scenes in the pictures and paintings make her long to be somewhere else. There are racks of pamphlets and flyers about pregnancy, caring for infants, teenagers and alcoholism, adults and alcoholism, child abuse, elder abuse, anger, depression, bullying, and drugs.

Anna fidgets in her seat as she tries not to think about

Christina. But it's of no use; her mind keeps going back to her friend. So many questions push their way into Anna's consciousness that she just can't avoid all of them. *What happened to Christina last night? Did DHHS investigate? If they did, did they remove her? Did they leave her there to suffer? Did they remove James? If they didn't show up, did James hurt her again?* That last question plagues Anna's thoughts horribly. She shudders as the horrible things that James has done to Christina fills her mind.

Just when Anna needs a distraction the most, a woman of average height and build and shoulder-length brown hair walks into the room. She is wearing dark blue slacks and a billowy white blouse with matching dark blue flowers. What catches Anna's attention the most is the woman's smile. This smile makes Anna feel that everything is going to be okay.

"Hello, you must be Sarah and Anna. My name is Valerie, and I talked to you on the phone yesterday," the lady says to Sarah. After shaking hands and exchanging minor comments about the how each of them is doing, Valerie leads the two down a hallway to a small office. The room is bright and cheery, which helps Anna's nervousness. Before Valerie sits in a chair behind a modest desk with a computer monitor in one corner, she instructs Sarah and Anna to sit in two of the three chairs on the other side of the desk.

Valerie looks at Anna and says, "I realize that you may have many questions that you want to ask me today." Anna simply nods her head and waits for her opportunity to speak. "Before we begin, I have to explain some things to you. First, any and all information that I have now or may gather later about Christina and her family is confidential, and I can't share that with you. Do you understand?" Anna isn't sure why Valerie can't give her information about her friend. *After all, wasn't I the one who gave them the information about Christina in the first place?*

"Why not?" Anna simply asks.

"Well, that is a good question, Anna. The answer lies in the law. You see, it's illegal for me to share confidential information about a person without that person's or his or her legal guardian's permission. Confidential information is personal information that can identify a person, such as his or her name, date of birth, social security number, address, phone number, and even incidents that have occurred in their lives," Valerie answers.

Before Valerie can continue, Anna says, "I know I'm repeating myself, but why?"

Valerie reassuringly smiles at Anna and says, "In the past, people have used this information to hurt others. I know you would never do anything to hurt Christina, at least not on purpose. Suppose, as you believe, that *someone*—Valerie holds up her hands and, with the first two fingers on each hand, makes quotation marks in the air as she says *someone*—"is hurting Christina and Christina is moved out of her home and away from that *someone* and we give you Christina's new address and phone number. *Someone,* through his parents, finds out that you have been in contact with Christina. *Someone* catches you alone and demands that you give him Christina's new address and phone number."

Anna angrily jumps in and says, "I'd never give it to him!" Anna slightly calms down as Valerie gives her another reassuring smile and nods her head in agreement.

"I do believe you would take that information to your grave," Valerie says supportingly.

"Yes I would," Anna says.

Valerie, still calmly smiling, says, "That's the problem, Anna." Anna looks at Valerie, dumbfounded. Valerie continues. "If *someone* knows for a fact that you know the information *someone* wants, *someone* may just be desperate enough to hurt you to get it."

Time in the little office stops. Anna hears one loud clunk as the second hand of the clock on the wall sounds, and then it doesn't move again for what seems like an eternity. Twice she looks from Valerie to her mother and back before she hears it clunk again. *Could James be capable of such a thing? Christina said he threatened to kill anyone she told*, Anna thinks to herself. Several seconds pass this way until, like a flash, time speeds up to normal. Before Anna can voice the thoughts she has just had, Valerie, sensing her near panic, says, "It's because of this and reasons like it that we must protect the safety of everyone through confidentiality. I do not believe that *someone* would do anything like that; however, we have to be safe."

Very frustrated and a bit angry, Anna quickly asks, "Then how will I know if Christina is safe? How do I find out if anything has been done to protect her from James? How will I know where she is?"

Valerie calmly smiles and says, "Anna, when you reported the abuse that was occurring to Christina, who did you do that for?"

Anna, thinking that this is the stupidest question she has ever been asked, huffily says, "Christina!"

Valerie, still smiling, says, "Yes, and as much as we want to meet your needs of concern, we must meet Christina's needs for safety and privacy first. I understand that you want to make sure that your friend is going to be okay. Unfortunately, you can't do that in any further way than you have already, and this part of the process is out of your control. You have done your job wonderfully in all of this, but the rest is up to others."

Anna feels her face become hot as she thinks about how she has been putting her needs before those of Christina. Anna, embarrassed by her actions, sheepishly says, "I'm sorry." Valerie, looking very serious extends her hand out across her desk to Anna. Anna hesitantly takes it.

Valerie looks directly into Anna's eyes while gently caressing her hand and very sincerely says, "Don't be. If all people had friends like you, there'd be less sadness in the world."

"Now that you know what I can't tell you, let me fill you in on what I can," Valerie says. "There will be an investigation into the allegations of abuse. That means that Christina will be asked questions by an investigator and a state patrol officer. Both of Christina's parents will be interviewed to find out if they are aware of any past or present abuse. And finally, Christina's brother will be questioned. If the investigator determines that abuse has occurred and Christina is still at risk for further abuse, one of several things may occur. One, depending on the response from Christina's parents, she may remain in the home and her abuser removed."

"Depending on what?" Anna asks.

"If Christina's parents know that abuse has been occurring and have not done anything to protect her," Valerie explains, "they will not be trusted to care for her now, and she will be removed and placed in a foster home. If one is not readily available, then she will be sent to a temporary shelter until one becomes available. Any questions so far?"

Both Sarah and Anna shake their heads.

"Secondly," Valerie says, "there are only a few foster homes that will take in teenagers. This means that if placement in a foster home is in the best interest of Christina, she will go to the first foster home available. That means she could be sent to live in a different town. This, as you can guess, can have both positive and negative meanings. It would be positive in that she would be safe from those who would harm her and negative because she would not be close to those that care about her."

"Is there a chance that I will be able to keep in contact with Christina?" Anna asks.

"That depends on the cooperation of Christina's parents; if they show signs of being supportive of

Christina, then she will stay in their care. If not, then she will be removed and the contact between Christina and anyone she has known in her past will be up to the discretion of her caseworker."

With the same calming smile, Valerie seriously says, "Anna, you need to understand something. Now, I'm not a therapist, but I've worked with hundreds of children who have been abused in one way or another. Each person is an individual, and yet they all have several things in common. They all are scared, hurt, confused, and angry about being abused, why they were abused, whose fault the abuse was, being taken from their homes and family, losing friends and having to make new ones, how their friends and family treat them, and just about everything else you can think of. They feel these emotions toward everyone, including their abuser, their family, their friends, their teachers, their caseworker, and their therapist. The more that they go through, the more intense these feelings become. I need you to know that

Christina may be very angry with you for a while."

With tears in her eyes and a lump in her throat, Anna says, "I know. I mean, I've been thinking about that ever since Christina first told me what happened to her. I knew I had to do something. I also knew that by telling I could lose her friendship. Even though I told Christina that I couldn't promise not to tell, it still feels like I've betrayed her. Do you know what I mean?" Anna sniffles as she wipes away the tears that have slowly rolled down her cheeks.

"She's so afraid that if James finds out and nothing is done to protect her, he'll do worse things to her for telling. Telling me! So it'll be my fault for telling. If that happens, she will hate me and herself forever." Valerie hands Anna a tissue from the box sitting on her desk. After blowing her nose, Anna calmly continues and says, "I guess I hadn't thought about her being taken from her home. If she is, I only hope that the person moving her explains to her why she is being moved and that it isn't her fault, that she's not being punished. As much as it might hurt to lose Christina as a friend"—Anna takes a deep breath and slowly lets it out—"I've got to take the chance to help her." Sarah reaches over, puts her arm around Anna, and gives her a reassuring smile that says not only "It's going to be okay," but also, "I'm very proud of you."

Valerie cannot help but admire this courageous young girl and thinks to herself, *Anna is so willing to be selfless. Normally a child in Anna's situation would not have told anyone for fear of losing a friend, but not Anna. No, this wonderful young lady cares so much for her friend that she's willing to lose that friend forever just to save her.*

Valerie swallows hard to get the lump in her throat to go away and then says, "Anna, there's not much more I can tell you at this time except that if Christina remains in her home you will, more than likely, see her at school. If you do not see her at school, you can believe that she is in a foster home in a new neighborhood.

Chapter 8

The Investigation

Christina arrives at school feeling better since talking to Anna the day before. Feeling less burdened and even happy, she is wearing more normal clothes, meaning tighter-fitting pink sweatpants instead of the usual extra-large faded blue jeans, and a blue T-shirt two sizes too big instead of the oversized, dirty black sweatshirt she usually wears. Her hair washed and pulled back out of her eyes, Christina is now completely visible. She sees that people are staring at her, and for the first time in a long time she's glad, and she smiles as people notice her.

Hoping to find Anna and let her know how much better she feels after breaking the silence of her abuse,

Christina searches the common areas where students hang out before school starts. Not having found Anna before the first bell of the day and feeling slightly disappointed but not defeated, Christina cheerfully walks to her first class.

She likes all the attention from people complimenting her all morning, but it's more than she is used to. She has an overwhelming desire to hide from everyone again. It doesn't help that she still has not seen Anna, the one person who completely understands and supports her. Near lunchtime, Christina's good mood is seriously tested.

The lunch bell rings, and Christina quickly gathers her books into her backpack. She leaves the classroom and enters the hallway, looking for Anna. Many people smile at Christina as she traverses the corridors to her locker. John, the most popular boy in school, walks right up to her and says, "Wow, you look great! Whatever it is that you're doing, keep it up!"

Christina instantly feels a rush of several emotions, and although she manages to say, "Th—th—thank you," she is not sure if she means it. She has had a crush on John for as long as she can remember and would give anything to have him talk to her. But not like this—not out of pity for the recovering sick person. *I know he's just being nice. Why is he being nice? Why is everyone being so nice? I know I look different today. But what, do they think I had the plague and suddenly, miraculously, have been cured? I've got news for them; I'm still the same person on the inside I've been on the outside. It sure was nice to have John smile at me though, even if it was out of pity. Wow, just thinking about it makes me melt. I can't wait to tell Anna. Where is she, anyway? If I don't find her at lunch, I'm going to the office to ask about her.*

The cafeteria is unusually crowded, and although Christina fervently searches, she just cannot find Anna. Finally she gives up her search and decides to eat some lunch. *I'll go to the office after lunch and see if they can tell me whether Anna is in school or not,* Christina thinks to herself. *I hope I didn't upset her.*

The latter thought starts to work on Christina like a tiny hole in a dam wall. One thought about Anna and where she is, and suddenly the dam begins to crack and she is overwhelmed with thoughts. *Did I scare her? Did I freak her out? Did I hurt her? I did hurt her. I don't deserve a friend like Anna. I'm so stupid for telling.* Other self-destructive thoughts burst from the dam and fill her mind until she finally ignores the onrush of thoughts and says, "No, I don't know what is going on with Anna, and until I do, I'm not going to blame myself, at least not yet!"

For the moment, Christina is able to patch the crack and stop up the tiny hole. However, she has lost her appetite to the deluge of negative thoughts. So she decides to dump her tray and go to the office.

Feeling good about being able to stop the cycle of negative thoughts, Christina walks into the office with a smile on her face. The secretary, Mrs. Jacobson, looks up from her desk and jokingly says, "Wow, you must have ESP; I was just going to page you." Mrs. Jacobson is a bubbly person with bright blue eyes and sandy blond hair. Always joking, she is liked by all the kids. Before she can ask why Mrs. Jacobson was going to page her, Christina hears someone say her name. Looking up, she sees a police officer through the window of the principal's office door, and her smile quickly fades.

A huge knot the size of a bowling ball fills her stomach as her knees begin to feel weak. Her hands begin to shake, and she starts sweating. From a distance she can hear the muffled voice of someone talking. She tries to concentrate on the voice and finally discovers that it is Mrs. Jacobson's. Christina shakes her head as if to clear cotton out of her ears and strains to listen.

Getting up from her desk and walking over to Christina, Mrs. Jacobson reaches an arm around Christina's shoulders and says, "It's going to be okay, sweetie. You're not in any trouble. Officer Donaldson and the Child Protective Service worker are only here to ask you some questions." Christina looks into the principal's office past the officer and finds a neatly dressed woman sitting in one of the chairs. Christina's heart nearly jumps out of her chest as she thinks, *Oh my God! They know!* Her own words echo through her mind. *What do I do now?* Just as suddenly as those thoughts come to her, she also realizes that they know because of Anna. *How could she? She's supposed to be my friend! That*—Christina's thought is interrupted as Officer Donaldson steps out of the principal's office and says, "Christina Stanly?"

Christina, still shocked by everything that's happening, just nods her head in agreement.

"Great! Would you please come in here with me?" Officer Donaldson gently asks. Christina thinks she is shaking her head, but finds herself walking toward the officer. As she gets closer, she realizes that he is tall and muscular and a bit intimidating in his uniform.

It's like everything is fuzzy, thinks Christina. She hears the officer introduce himself and ask her to sit down. She understands what he wants, but cannot make out exactly what he is saying. She sits down and blankly stares at the woman across from her. Christina knows that she is being introduced to the woman, and yet she cannot remember her name. Christina thinks to herself, *How funny, they all sound like the teacher from the old Charlie Brown cartoons. Blah blah. Blah blah. Blah, blah, blah, blah.* Although this is interesting to her, it seems totally incredible that she's able to respond and answer their questions.

Christina tries to tune into what she is saying to the woman and the officer, but the fuzz is too thick to break through. Christina thinks, *What am I saying to these people? I need to shut up! Shut up! Come on, shut up! Why can't I control myself?* Finally she yells, "Hey! Shut up!" Yelling at herself makes her fuzziness go away, and she looks up and notices that Officer Donaldson and the woman are puzzled. "Oh, did I say that out loud?"

The woman, Annette Peters, gently nods her head and smiles kindly. Annette realizes that Christina, who had been answering all of their questions with great detail but with absolutely no emotion, had been disassociating to protect herself. Christina's yelling at herself to shut up only confirms Annette's suspicions. Annette calmly and gently asks, "Christina, are you aware that you have been here talking to us for almost an hour now?" Christina jerks her head toward the clock on the wall. In total amazement and disbelief, she reads 1:45. *It can't be,* she thought. *I just sat down. How could I have been here for that long? It was only 12:50 when I walked in the office to ask about Anna, and now it's almost an hour later.*

"It's okay," Annette says reassuringly. "Many abuse victims mentally disconnect themselves when they are experiencing bad things. You do need to know that you have told us all about the abuse that has occurred to you, and you do not have to repeat it again right now." Christina sighs heavily in relief that it is over, at least for now.

Chapter 9

Family Secrets

Being told that she didn't have to talk about the abuse anymore, and figuring that she would be allowed to go to class, Christina stands up and starts toward the door.

"Christina?" Annette says. "Um, we're not quite done here yet."

Christina, being both confused and irritated, says, "I thought you said I wouldn't have to talk about anything anymore?"

"That's correct; I did say that, and I meant it. However, your parents are on their way here for Officer Donaldson and me to talk to and to possibly take you home," Annette explains.

Christina's head begins to swim, and she screams, "No! No! No! You can't tell them! They will never believe it. James is perfect. Don't you get it? They'll blame me."

Annette tries to interrupt Christina by saying, "Calm down—"

She is unable to finish, as Christina yells over her voice, "How stupid are you people? Don't you think that if I thought my parents would understand I would've told them a long time ago about what's been happening to me? I know them, and they won't handle this well. They're going to hate me!" Christina is pacing back and forth as she raves. With her last statement, she sits down and begins to cry. Annette attempts to tell Christina not to assume anything and to reassure her that things are going to get better. The news of her parents finding out is too much for her to handle, and as suddenly as before, Christina's fuzziness returns and she doesn't understand anything that Annette is saying.

No longer crying, Christina comes out of her fuzziness to discover that Mrs. Jacobson is sitting next to her, rubbing her shoulders in a soothing way. She also notices that Officer Donaldson and Annette are no longer there. She turns to Mrs. Jacobson and says, "Where'd they go?" Mrs. Jacobson points a finger toward the vice-principal's office. Christina gasps as she sees her parents through the office window.

Mr. Stanly is standing behind his wife with his hands on her shoulders as Annette tells them about their children. Mr. Stanly is a tall man, standing six feet, two inches tall. He is slender, with rugged good looks and dark brown hair. Mrs. Stanly looks a great deal like Christina, only with lighter brown hair and softer features.

After finishing their conversation, Annette leads Mr. and Mrs. Stanly out of the vice-principal's office and across the front office to the principal's office. As they enter the room, Christina jumps to her feet and takes a couple of steps backward. Everyone sees the terror on Christina's face as she anticipates her parents' reaction. Mrs. Stanly instantly places her hands over her mouth, and begins to cry as she sees the horror on her daughter's face. She walks over to Christina and reassuringly reaches out her arms to hug her. Christina, still cautious, allows her mother to hug her. As soon as Mrs. Stanly wraps her arms around Christina, Christina says, "Please don't hate me!" and she breaks down and begins to cry. The stress and the pressure of the moment cause the fuzz to begin to creep up on Christina again. She puts all her effort into focusing on listening.

"Oh baby, I could never hate you. I love you!" Mrs. Stanly says, trying not to lose control, but still crying. "I'm so sorry, honey. I didn't know that this was going on. If I had, I promise you I'd have done something to keep you safe. You see, James was sexually abused by your uncle Roger when he went to stay with them when he was twelve. Do you remember that summer? You were seven, and you cried and cried because you didn't get to go too."

Christina, trying to keep the fuzz at bay, concentrates and says, "James was abused? Why didn't you do anything? I mean, why didn't you take him to therapy or something?"

"He said he was fine, sweetie," Mr. Stanly gets down on one knee in front of Christina, and takes her hand. "He's been doing very well in school and sports and has a part-time job. He has good friends that don't get into trouble. We thought he would be fine. Until today, we thought he was fine." Mr. Stanly, pausing, glances down for a moment. Looking up with tears in his eyes he says, "I am so very sorry, honey. If I'd known what could've happened, I would have done everything in my power to protect you. I promise that we will get both of you all the help you need. Your mom and I will cut back on our time at work. We'll go to counseling with you. And most importantly, we'll keep you safe in your own home."

"What about James?" Christina blurts out.

Mrs. Stanly quickly says, "Your father and I let James down by not getting him the help he needs. We recognize that he can't be in our home with you—not until he realizes that what he has done has been wrong and he proves that he can be trusted again. Don't worry, baby; we are still going to love him and try to help him the best we can. It just won't be at home." With that, Christina breaks down and starts crying. Mr. and Mrs. Stanly, also crying, lean in and hug their daughter.

***

An hour later, across town at Central High School, State Patrol Officer Donaldson and Child Protective Service Investigator Annette Peters are having a conversation with James.

Being the charismatic person that he is, James smiles

and answers Annette's questions as calmly as he can. He denies ever having had any kind of sexual contact with Christina. But when Annette continues to ask more specific questions, James begins to lose his cool. He makes minor mistakes as he tries to blame sexual contact with his sister on Christina herself. He says, "It's her fault. She wanted to have sex and wanted me to teach her how."

Annette asks calmly, "James, didn't you just say that you had never had sexual contact with Christina?"

James's frustration increases as he realizes that he is not convincing, and sounding defeated, he says yes and asks, "Okay, if I tell you the truth, what's going to happen to me?" As soothingly as she can, Anette explains to James that he is going to be staying at Kenworth's Home for Boys for a short time until they can get him into a treatment home specifically for adolescent sex offenders. The more he is willing to own up to his actions and take responsibility for them, the sooner he can return home.

James spends the next two hours describing in detail everything that he either did to Christina or made her do to him. Annette also asks him to talk about the abuse he has suffered at the hands of his uncle Roger. This is very difficult for James to do, but in the end he manages to tell her everything.

Annette compliments James for telling her the truth and asks him to stay seated as she leaves the room. She quickly returns with two other people following her. As he recognizes his parents, James's mood quickly changes from relief to shame. He wishes he could disappear.

Mr. and Mrs. Stanly calmly walk across the room to where James is sitting. Instead of the disappointment James expects to find in their voices, he hears love and concern. He gingerly looks up into their expecting eyes and finds acceptance. "James," Mr. Stanly begins. "We know everything that has been happening. Your mother and I are going to do everything we can to help you and your sister. I'm very sorry that we didn't get you the help you needed after what Roger did to you. But we are going to make up for that now. Son, I love you very much, and I want you to get better."

Mrs. Stanly quietly says, "Honey, I'm not mad at you for what you have done to Christina. I am very concerned for both of you. I'm going to be right here for you the whole way. But you need to know that I'm going to be there for Christina as well. Okay?"

In shock that his parents have not yelled at him, disowned him, or worse, tried to kill him, he simply nods his head in agreement. "Am I still going to Kenworth?" James asks. Both Mr. and Mrs. Stanly nod their heads in confirmation.

Mr. Stanly says, "Yes, son, for the time being, anyway. It wouldn't be fair to you to put you back in a situation in which you would be tempted to repeat your actions without knowing how to control yourself. And it wouldn't be fair for Christina to put her at risk of being abused again."

"I promise I won't do anything to her. Please don't let them take me," begs James.

"James, this is the best thing right now. We'll call you every day and come and see you as often as we can. You need to understand just how important it is for you to get the help you need right way. If you truly are sorry for what you have done, then you understand this is the best way to help yourself and your sister," Mrs. Stanly softly yet sternly says.

Realizing that he cannot win the argument, James, subdued, agrees to go to Kenworth even though he is not truly sorry for what he has done.

Chapter 10

Not Out of the Woods Yet

The doorbell sounds. "I'll get it!" screams Saddie from the kitchen. The front entrance opens into the living room, and Anna, being in the living room, watching television, gets up and starts for the door. Saddie yells, "I said I'd get it," and begins to run to the door. Anna, feeling like aggravating her sister, decides to race her to the door. Saddie is yelling, "No, no, no. That's not fair; I called it first." Just before they get to the door, Anna stops and lets Saddie go past her.

With a giant smile on her face, Saddie swings open the door to greet a person that she has never seen before. "Oops, I'm not supposed to open the door for strangers," says Saddie.

"That's a really good idea," Valerie says, smiling. Saddie smiles and slams the door shut in Valerie's face. Playing along, Valerie rings the bell again. This time, before opening the door, Saddie asks, "Who is it?"

"Valerie Smith from the Department of Health and Human Services," is the reply.

"Just a minute, please," Saddie shouts at the door. Saddie turns to Anna and asks, "Do you know this person—Valerie?"

"Yes, Saddie, she's the lady Mom and I went to talk to about Christina," Anna says.

Saddie opens the door and confidently says, "Please come in, Valerie Smith, of the Department of Health and Human Services."

Valerie does as she is bid with a very broad smile across her face. She enters the living room and greets

Anna, who has a look on her face that says "My sister is a dork." Anna leads Valerie into the kitchen, where Sarah is just finishing up the dishes. After polite greetings, Valerie asks if she can talk with both Anna and Sarah. The three of them take seats around the kitchen table.

"Would you care for something to drink, Valerie?" Sarah asks. "We have soda, tea, milk, and water." Valerie thanks Sara but declines the offer.

"Let me start with Mrs. Davis," Valerie says. "Mr. and Mrs. Stanly informed the Child Protective Services investigator that Mrs. Davis contacted them and told them that you, Anna, had made allegations to her that James was sexually molesting Christina."

Surprised, Anna says, "She didn't!"

Valerie nods her head and says, "Yes, she did."

Sarah, concerned, says, "Isn't that against the code of ethics for her profession?"

"I'm not one hundred percent sure at this moment," says Valerie. "I know it is for a licensed mental health counselor, but as for a school counselor, I'm not sure. Anyway, she might be able to disguise it as a duty to warn, which mental health counselors give. However, according to Mr. and Mrs. Stanly, she was not warning them on Christina's behalf; she tried to warn them on James's behalf, saying that he was being falsely accused."

Anna, having a sinking feeling, asks, "How does that affect things?"

"Well, it only affects Mrs. Davis herself," Valerie says boldly. "You see, the truth is out. Both Christina and James have admitted to what we feel is everything. That means that Mrs. Davis is going to have to face a formal investigation into her actions on this case and possibly her interactions with all children at this school."

"Some more good news is that because of Mrs. Davis's blunder, Mr. and Mrs. Stanly know of your involvement and have signed a consent to release information form, allowing you to be notified of how things are going and being handled, Anna," Valerie says cheerfully.

"Really? That's great," Anna happily shouts.

Valerie begins to fill Anna and Sarah in on Christina's interview. She does not go into all of the details of the abuse, but she lets them know that Christina was very cooperative with the investigator and the state patrol officer. Upon hearing that there was an officer present, Anna feels sorry for her friend. Valerie describes how Mr. and Mrs. Stanly supported their daughter and how they all hugged each other when it was over.

Next Valerie tells them about James's interview and how he denied everything at first. Thinking to herself— *that jerk, how could he do that to Christina? It's bad enough that he hurt her, but to deny it ... ugh!* This makes Anna very mad, and she begins to cry. Both Sarah and Valerie console her by patting her shoulder and touching her hand. Valerie continues and explains how the investigator was able to get James to confess. She also explains how Mr. and Mrs. Stanly were able to support James even though he had hurt Christina.

The two biggest questions on Anna's mind had not been answered yet. Not being one to hold back, Anna asks Valerie, "What happened to Christina and James? Are they staying in the same home?"

Valerie smiles and says, "Christina is remaining in her home with her parents. She will continue to attend the same school. She will begin seeing a therapist both individually and with her parents. James will be staying at Kenworth's Home for Boys until he can be placed in a treatment center for adolescent perpetrators." Anna lets out a huge sigh that sounds like she had been holding it since Christina first told her all about the abuse.

"Anna, we're not out of the woods yet," Valerie says very matter-of-factly.

"What do you mean?" asks Anna.

Valerie seriously says, "There is a great deal of work ahead of these people—not only a lot of work for Christina and James, but for their parents as well. I feel confident that if the Stanly family sticks to what they believe right now, they'll do fine. But if they fall back into avoiding their responsibilities, then I'm not so sure of their odds. Also, Anna, do you remember telling me that you knew that Christina was going to be mad at you?" Valerie asks.

"Yes," Anna reluctantly responds.

"Well, unfortunately you were right," Valerie says. "I believe that this shall pass, but you're going to have to give her some time."

Feeling sure that Christina's abuse is at an end, Anna accepts responsibility for Christina's anger toward her and sets her mind to being patient. *I know she will come around someday if I just wait long enough; long enough for her to recognize that I did it out of love,* Anna confidently thinks.

***

Four months have passed since the day that Valerie visited, and still Anna has had no contact with Christina. Anna sent a Christmas card to Christina and her family, and yet Christina did not respond. Mr. and Mrs. Stanly sent Anna a very nice letter thanking her for coming forward soon after the interview. They continue to write to her a couple of times a month and let her know how Christina and James are doing. Anna writes them back faithfully, thanking them for keeping her informed, but what she really wants is for Christina to talk to her herself.

Although Anna is disappointed that Christina has not spoken to her yet, she is very happy to see the improvement in Christina's attitude. Christina is talking to other students and back to dressing in a more liberal manner. Anna has not approached Christina for fear of pushing her away. She has waited for Christina to come to her.

It is February fourteenth, Valentine's Day, and everyone at school has been giving out boxes of chocolates, cards, and even flowers. It's ten o'clock and a free period for Anna, and she is sitting in the common room, reading her history lesson. The first time she realizes that someone is standing next to her is when she hears "Ahem." She looks up to see Christina gazing right at her. "Anna, before you say anything, I want you to listen to everything I have to say," says Christina. After seeing Anna nod in confirmation, she says, "I was really, really, really mad at you. I know you said that you couldn't keep my secret, but I never thought you'd tell, or at least not to anyone who would've done anything."

After taking a deep breath, Christina continues, saying, "After a while I started to get over being mad at you. Mostly because things were better between me and my parents and I wasn't being abused anymore. I still didn't trust you. I mean, I was afraid that I wouldn't be able to tell you anything without you blabbing it all over school. My therapist helped me understand why you told and that you did it out of caring for me. But by that time I didn't know how to approach you, and I was feeling guilty for the way I treated you."

Christina pauses and wipes the tears from her eyes and says, "I want so much for us to be friends again, Anna. I've so many things to tell you about. I hope you can forgive me for being angry and shutting you out." As Christina finishes her statement, she hands Anna a single long-stemmed red rose. Anna smiles brightly, snatches the rose out of Christina's hand, and lunges at her and gives her the biggest hug either of them has ever had.

Anna tells Christina that she forgives her and that she loves her, but because she is crying so hard, her words are unintelligible. After repeating her feelings so that Christina can understand them, Anna says, "BFF?"

Christina replies by saying, "BFFE—best friends for eternity!" Then says, "By the way, you'll never guess who likes me."

"Who?" Anna asks excitedly.

The End

If you or anyone you know is being hurt by someone, please call 1-800-4achild (1-800-422-4453), your local law-enforcement agency, your local social-services agency, or 911.

Helping a child ends generations of illness—past, present, and future. Please help a child today. – Dean Balderston, M.A. Ed. LMHP

Dean is a licensed mental health practitioner in the state of Nebraska. He has been helping children and families work through many of life's traumas since 2002. He is a trained eye-movement desensitization and reprocessing (EMDR) therapist since 2003. He has worked with many individuals suffering from sexual abuse, with great success. Dean has compiled information from the research of this book, and from the next book, to create two workshops. If you would like information about these workshops, or would like to contact Dean, please e-mail him at, eventswithdean@yahoo.com